The Secret Of The

Tooth Fairy

Twinkle Toes
Virginia Beach, Virginia

A SPECIAL GIFT

TO YOU

FROM

THE SECRET

OF THE
TOOTH FAIRY

Theresa Lee

Illustrations by
Diane Buckley

Library of Congress Catalog Card Number: 98-96244
ISBN: 0-9664625-0-5
ISBN: 0-9664625-1-3 (pbk.)

Illustrations by Diane Buckley
Graphic art logo by Percival Tesoro

Twinkle Toes Inc.
P.O. Box 65077
Virginia Beach, Virginia 23467
1-757-479-9363
1-877-2-Twinkle (toll free)
1-757-479-9369 (fax)
www.2twinkle.com

First Edition

"Never take for granted the small everyday wonders."

T. F.

The day began like any other Monday. Alyssa's Mom came into her room, turned on the light and said, "Good morning sunshine! Time to get ready for school."

Alyssa laid in bed awhile and stretched. She knew she better get up, so she started kicking off her covers. Suddenly her dog, Lady, jumped up on the bed with her tail a'wagging. Not wanting to be left out, her cat, Snuggles, hopped up too. He was purring like crazy and kept trying to get in between Lady and Alyssa. She couldn't help but giggle at the two of them.

It certainly did seem like a normal morning. Yet, Alyssa had the feeling something had changed. She just couldn't figure out what it was. Her Mom woke her up like she always does. Lady and Snuggles were right there with her while she was getting ready. Still, Alyssa was certain something was very different.

Alyssa got dressed and came into the kitchen for breakfast. When she took her first bite of cereal, she realized what was so special about today. It had finally happened! She had her first loose tooth! Right away Alyssa told her Mom the news.

"How exciting," her Mom said. "Of course, it will be awhile before your tooth actually falls out."

Well that didn't bother Alyssa. Her tooth was definitely loose. All the other kids in her first grade class had already lost at least one tooth. Now, at long last, she too would be visited by the Tooth Fairy. She could wait a few more days.

They finished getting ready and headed out the door to school. On the way a thought occurred to Alyssa. "Mom, what does the Tooth Fairy do with my tooth after she takes it?" she asked as they pulled up to the school.

"That's a good question honey," her Mom said. "I've never really thought about it before. Maybe it's just one of life's little mysteries. Now give me a kiss and go on into school."

Alyssa enjoyed school and always paid attention, but that day she had trouble listening. Once her teacher, Miss Randolph, even had to remind her to finish her class work. Alyssa kept wondering about the teeth that the Tooth Fairy gathers every night. When you think of all the children in the whole world, that's a lot of teeth!

At the end of school, the first graders stay with their teachers until their ride home comes. While Alyssa was waiting, she asked Miss Randolph about the Tooth Fairy.

"So that's what was on your mind today," Miss Randolph said with a smile. "Actually I haven't thought about it before. I don't know what she does with the teeth she collects."

She suggested Alyssa ask the school Librarian, Mrs. Brenzovich. Everyone calls her Mrs. B. Maybe she could find the answer in one of her books in the school library. Tuesday was library day for the first grade, so Alyssa could ask her tomorrow.

On Monday's, Alyssa had soccer practice with Coach Al. She loved to play soccer and Coach Al was so much fun. He could always get all the kids laughing during practice.

That night she was goalie for the practice game. She was usually a pretty good goalie, but this time she missed several easy plays. She couldn't stop thinking about all those teeth! At the end of practice she decided to see if Coach Al knew what happens to your tooth after the Tooth Fairy takes it.

"Alyssa, I don't have any idea what she does with your tooth," he told her. "Now that you bring it up, I'd really like to know myself. I bet it's a secret that only she knows, but if you ever find out would you please tell me?"

Alyssa promised him she would.

While Alyssa was lying in bed that night, she kept wiggling her tooth with her tongue. Her Daddy came to tuck her in and she asked him about the Tooth Fairy's secret. She told him she had asked Mom, Miss Randolph and even Coach Al, but so far nobody knew.

"Well, I don't know either pumpkin," her Dad said. "I never thought about it when I was a little boy. Why don't I look on the computer tonight and see if I can find the answer there." Then he snugged the covers around her and kissed her goodnight.

Alyssa went to sleep right after her Dad left. She was sure that he would be able to tell her the answer tomorrow morning. Her Daddy's computer had so much stuff in it, she just knew he'd learn the secret there.

The first thing she did the next morning was ask her Mom if Daddy had found out the Tooth Fairy's secret. Her Mom said her Dad tried and tried to find it on the computer, but it wasn't there. Alyssa was disappointed, but maybe Mrs. B could help her find the answer today in the library.

On Tuesdays, Miss Randolph's class went to the library right after lunch. Alyssa always looked forward to going, but this Tuesday she couldn't hardly wait. Mrs. B has a zillion books, one of them must have the answer. Alyssa checked with her as soon as they got to the library.

"Well that's a new question," Mrs. B said. "Let's check the card catalog and see if we have any books about the Tooth Fairy." They looked and found two books, but neither one said what happens to your tooth.

The days went by and Alyssa's tooth wiggled more and more. She didn't ask anyone else about the Tooth Fairy's secret. No one knew the answer. It seemed to her that she was the only one who really cared. She tried to be like everyone else and just not think about it anymore. Except that sometimes, in the quiet of her room just before she went to sleep, she would find herself still wondering.

Then finally one day it happened. She bit into a slice of pizza and her tooth fell out. Tonight would be the night! Tonight the Tooth Fairy would come into her room while she was sleeping and take her tooth out from under her pillow.

Bedtime came and Alyssa folded a tissue around her tooth. Her Mom helped her put it in just the right spot under the pillow. She was excited about the Tooth Fairy coming, but she was also a little sad. This was the first baby tooth she would leave for the Tooth Fairy, and she would never know what happened to it.

Alyssa had trouble falling asleep that night, but finally drifted off. Just before she went to sleep, she wished one last time she could learn the secret of the Tooth Fairy.

In the middle of the night something woke Alyssa up. As she opened her eyes, she saw a soft golden light. The center of it sparkled like glitter. She couldn't see exactly where the light was coming from, but heard a beautiful voice. "Alyssa, I understand that you've tried very hard to learn my secret."

It was the Tooth Fairy! Somehow Alyssa knew not to be afraid. "Yes," she answered "but I never did find out. It didn't seem to matter to anyone else but me."

There was a long silence. Then the Tooth Fairy told Alyssa, "Since you have wanted to know more than anyone else ever has, I've decided to tell my secret just this one time. You may share it with others, but I'll not speak of it again.

"You see my sweet child, it's really very simple. There is magic in the laughter of all small children. Every time you laugh, a little piece of that magic is left in your baby teeth.

"This is why your teeth are so precious to me. I use them to make my magic fairy dust. Then every night as I travel from house to house, I scatter it all around the world. It's my fairy dust that puts the *special* into the wonderful little everyday things that make people smile.

"When a puppy wags its tail or a kitten purrs, people can't help but smile. Think of the fluttering of a butterfly's wings as it passes by, a dolphin as it jumps up out of the ocean, the light of the fireflies on a hot summer night and the colors of the rainbow against a pale blue sky. They each have a bit of magic because I've added the pureness of a child's joy.

"Please remember this when you find yourself smiling at the simple beauty of life. Never take for granted the small everyday wonders.

"I must go now. Tomorrow morning you will find a special gift from me in exchange for your tooth. This gift is to help remind you of my secret, and how important your laughter is to me."

The next morning Alyssa's Mom turned on her light and said, "Good morning sunshine, time to get up and get ready for school."

Before Alyssa had barely opened her eyes, she remembered what had happened last night! She now knew the wonderful secret of the Tooth Fairy. It was a night she would cherish forever. She couldn't imagine what her other gift from the Tooth Fairy was.

Alyssa gingerly reached under her pillow and felt the softness of velvet. She gently pulled out a beautiful small pouch. She knew the Tooth Fairy had given her this special gift to use every time she left a tooth under her pillow. Alyssa would never forget that a child's laughter is precious and holds a marvelous treasure.

Just then, Lady jumped up wagging her tail and was immediately followed by a purring Snuggles. She smiled as she petted them. Yes, she finally knew the secret of the Tooth Fairy, and would always think of it when she smiled at the wonderful little everyday things of life.

Theresa Lee Litalien, native of Virginia, grew up in Roanoke which is nestled at the foothills of the Blue Ridge Mountains. Graduated from Virginia Tech with a degree in Business Management. Currently an insurance professional in Virginia and lives in Chesapeake with husband and daughter.

Diane Buckley, native of Vermont, studied illustration at the Columbus College of Art and Design in Columbus, Ohio. Graduated from the Art Institute of Pittsburgh. Currently teaching in Virginia and lives in Suffolk with husband and three teenage daughters.